"HELLO READING books are a perfect introduction to reading. Brief sentences full of word repetition and full-color pictures stress visual clues to help a child take the first important steps toward reading. Mastering these storybooks will build children's reading confidence and give them the enthusiasm to stand on their own in the world of words."

—Bee Cullinan
Past President of the International Reading
Association, Professor in New York University's
Early Childhood and Elementary Education Program

"Readers aren't born, they're made. Desire is planted—planted by parents who work at it."

—Jim Trelease
author of *The Read-Aloud Handbook*

When I was a classroom reading teacher, I recognized the importance of good stories in making children understand that reading is more than just recognizing words. I saw that children who have ready access to storybooks get excited about reading. They also make noticeably greater gains in reading comprehension. The development of the HELLO READING stories grows out of this experience."

—Harriet Ziefert
M.A.T., New York University School of Education
Author, Language Arts Module,
Scholastic Early Childhood Program

Emma
Sam
Anna

VIKING
Published by the Penguin Group
Viking Penguin, a division of Penguin Books USA Inc.,
375 Hudson Street, New York, New York 10014, U.S.A.
Penguin Books Ltd, 27 Wrights Lane, London W8 5TZ, England
Penguin Books Australia Ltd, Ringwood, Victoria, Australia
Penguin Books Canada Ltd, 2801 John Street, Markham, Ontario, Canada L3R 1B4
Penguin Books (N.Z.) Ltd, 182-190 Wairau Road, Auckland 10, New Zealand

Penguin Books Ltd, Registered Offices: Harmondsworth, Middlesex, England

First published in 1991 by Viking Penguin, a division of Penguin Books USA Inc.

1 3 5 7 9 10 8 6 4 2

Text copyright © Fred Ehrlich, 1991
Illustrations copyright © Martha Gradisher, 1991
All rights reserved
Library of Congress catalog card number: 90-50422
ISBN 0-670-84274-5

Printed in Singapore for Harriet Ziefert, Inc.

A VALENTINE
FOR MS. VANILLA

Fred Ehrlich
Pictures by Martha Gradisher

VIKING

4/22/

It's Valentine's Day.

Ms. Vanilla puts
a Valentine box
on her desk.

"Now, class," she says, "we will make Valentines."

Everybody gets busy.
Very busy.

They all make cards.

They all write poems.

One, two, three, four, five—
the box is stuffed with Valentines.

"Now, class," says Ms. Vanilla,
"it's cleanup time. Clean up.
Then we can have our party."

It's party time in
Ms. Vanilla's class.

Angelina gives out napkins.
Charlene gives out cupcakes.

Donald gives out candy hearts.

And Ms. Vanilla
pours the punch.

"Now, class," says Ms. Vanilla,
"it's time to open Valentines.
Lee Wong, you can pick first."

Lee Wong opens a card.

He reads:

I will cover you with slime
If you won't be my Valentine!

Mary Ann opens a card.
She reads:

I'll be your Valentine, I think,
If you stop telling me I stink.

Donald reads his.

Valentine, you mean more to me
Than watching cartoons on my TV.

Charlene reads hers.

Valentine, I'll stick to you,
Like chewing gum upon my shoe.

Everyone listens to Angelina.

My Valentine is never icky,
Like oatmeal
When it's cold and sticky.

Next comes Paul.

Valentine, you're not so good to eat,
But still I think you're pretty neat.

Now it's Ben's turn.

I'll climb on Ms. Vanilla's desk,
If my Valentine says
She loves me best.

Melba is last.

Roses are red, violets are blue,
Kiss Ms. Vanilla and I'll kiss you.

Then Rosa says, "Ms. Vanilla, we made a Valentine for you."

For Ms. Vanilla we all cheer,
The greatest teacher of the year.
Here's a heart we all have signed—
Will you be our Valentine?

Angelina Benita

MaryAnn

Max Charlene Ben

Paul

Rosa Harry

Donald